Animal
Adventures

Written by Fiona Conboy ——————— Illustrated by Manhar Chauhan

SIENA

Percival's Tail

Percival the peacock was a beautiful bird, there was absolutely no doubt about that, and everyone loved it when he fanned out his tail feathers and gave them the most wonderful, colourful display. But one day Percival woke up and found he had a problem. "Oh no!" he cried, "My tail feathers have stuck– I can't do a thing with them!"

"Dear me," said the robin, "that's terrible. I wonder how it happened?" Percival didn't care how it had happened, all *he* cared about was trying to get his tail fixed. "I mean," he said, "what good is a peacock who can't fan out his tail–I might as well be a chicken!" Clarice, the chicken, was a little put out by this comment.

She thought being a chicken was a very nice thing to be, but even she agreed that a peacock who couldn't fan out his tail feathers was a very sad thing indeed.

Some time later they crept back and sneaked up behind Percival. Phil silently blew up a large brown paper bag and as he popped it, Robin yelled

"SURPRISE!!"

Sure enough, Percival was so surprised that his fabulous tail feathers shot up in the air. "That's the best surprise I've ever had!" grinned Percival.

Try as they might, none of the animals could come up with a solution.
"I'm stumped," said Robin.
"I'm clucked if I know what to do," said Clarice.
"I'm bound to say I haven't a single idea," said Ronald Rabbit. Percival was a very unhappy peacock. Later that day Phil the fox whispered to Robin "I've got an idea!" and the two of them tip-toed off together.

Lawrence to the Rescue

Lawrence got his big red balloon ready for the journey to the South Pole. "We're off!" they cried as the balloon climbed up into the sky, and it wasn't long before they reached the South Pole. "Look," cried Billy, "there he is!" Blue Whale was lying on the ice, beside a crowd of penguins. "We're coming down!" Billy shouted.

Lawrence the polar bear was having breakfast one morning, when he heard a loud knock at his door. It was his friend, Billy, a penguin from the South Pole. "We need your help!" he puffed. "Blue Whale is stuck on the ice!"

With the penguins' help, Lawrence tied strong ropes around Blue Whale. "One, two, three, *lift off!*" The balloon began to rise in the air, and so did Blue Whale. "You'll be the world's first flying whale!" cheered the penguins.

"Thank you, Lawrence," sighed Blue Whale as he was lowered back into the water. Billy climbed out of the balloon. "See you all again soon, I hope!" called Lawrence, as he drifted off towards the North Pole. "But no more emergencies please!"

Jokes on Casper

There was nothing Casper the raccoon liked better than playing tricks on his friends, although, to be honest, his friends did not feel the same way. If there was one thing they were completely fed up with, it was having tricks played on them by Casper.

"If Casper moves my winter store of nuts one more time," said Sam squirrel, "I don't know what I'll do!" Everyone agreed, especially Thelma the turkey, because Casper had recently put a large pebble amongst her eggs and she'd spent ages trying to hatch it. "I think he deserves some of his own medicine," she said firmly . . .

"It's not that we don't like you, Casper," said Sam, when Casper asked him what was going on. "It's just that a joke's only funny when *everyone* laughs, d'you see?" Casper did see, and from then on he only told jokes, and all his friends really liked that.

The next morning Casper awoke to find his front door glued shut. When he finally got it open he discovered the milk on the doorstep was blue and when he poured out his cereal it wasn't cereal at all but wood shavings! When he put his shoes on he found his laces were missing, and then he noticed people giggling as he went past. Someone had pinned "Tease Me!" to the back of his jacket. "I'm fed up with this," Casper thought to himself. "Why is everyone playing tricks on me?"

Mickey's Rainy Day

The trouble was, Mickey had a cold and he didn't want to get wet. "It'll only get worse if I get wet," he told himself. "But if I stay here I can't go and see all my friends—what am I going to do?" Just then Terry the toucan flew past Mickey's tree. "Hello there, Mickey," he said, waving a wing at him. "There's a party over at Henry's—are you coming?"

Mickey the chimp was bored. He was sure he'd never been this bored before. It had been pouring with rain the whole morning and he hadn't been able to do anything. He tried going back to sleep but the sound of the rain on the banana leaf roof over his head kept him awake. "Is it *ever* going to stop raining?" he sighed.

Mickey couldn't believe it. He was going to have to miss the party!

He was trying to work out how he could get to Henry's party when he saw Tommy the turtle trundling by, his head tucked under his shell to keep it dry. "That gives me an idea!" said Mickey, looking round for some sticks, "I wonder if I can make it work..."

After a few false starts Mickey finally got it right—his idea did work! "I hope the party isn't over," he said as he swung down to the ground and scampered off towards Henry's house. He soon caught up with Tommy. Mickey looked up at the roof of leaves over his head. "I got the idea from you, Tommy," grinned Mickey, "I call it a bananarella!"

Pin Pin's Birthday Surprise

Pin Pin woke up feeling very hungry—his tummy was rumbling very loudly. But when he looked in his store of bamboo shoots he found it was completely empty. "I don't remember eating it all," he thought. "But I suppose I'd better go and find some more for breakfast," he said as he set off to look for some fresh, juicy bamboo shoots.

But wherever Pin Pin looked there was nothing to be found. "How odd," he said, "it looks as though someone's been here before me—but I can't think who. No one else round here likes bamboo shoots." Pin Pin carried on searching for the rest of the morning, but with no luck at all. He asked everyone he met if they'd seen anyone eating bamboo shoots, but no one could help him.

By lunchtime, Pin Pin wasn't just hungry–he was *starving!* "If I don't have something to eat soon," he said, "they will hear my stomach rumbling on the other side of the hill!" There was just one place left for Pin Pin to search when he saw Ricky beckoning to him. "I wonder what Ricky wants now?" thought Pin Pin. He followed Ricky into a little clearing and as Pin Pin turned the corner . . .

"HAPPY BIRTHDAY!" shouted all his friends, and before him lay the biggest pile of bamboo shoots he had ever seen. "We've been collecting them for you all morning," they said. "Tuck in!"

"Sorry," said Edward the eagle, "I haven't seen anything."
Ricky the rat was no help and neither was Pompey the pig.
"I wonder what's going on?" frowned Pin Pin. He didn't notice that all his friends were wearing the biggest grins ever.

Kevin loses his way

After a while Kevin felt very alone. "Maybe," he said to himself, "it's just possible that I *am* lost . . ." An hour later, as the sun was beginning to go down, Kevin *knew* he was lost. "And I'm going to be out here," said Kevin, quietly, "on my own . . . in the dark . . . *all* night."

"Are you sure you know the way, Kevin?" asked Bruce. The two koalas were walking along a track neither of them had been down before. They were looking for a really big eucalyptus tree that Kevin said he knew the way to. "Well it's getting late," said Bruce, turning to start back home, "and I think we're going to get lost if we carry on." Kevin said he was being silly, waved goodbye and carried on walking.